This book belongs to

_____

Communication Ninja

By Mary Nhin

Thank you for trusting me.

I understand.

Thank you for sharing with me.

I appreciate you.

Pictures by
Jelena Stupar

But then soon, communication had gone wrong between Angry Ninja and Hangry Ninja.

There's an easy way I remember these tips.

It's called the Communication C.L.U.E.

You can use any of them at any time in any order!

I **choose** positive words over negative ones.
For instance, "Don't sit there" becomes...

Please sit here.

Here's another example.

"You're not going the right way!" becomes...

It also helps me to put myself in the other person's shoes.

How would I feel if this happened to me?

Here's an easy chart showing how to use "I" more than "you":

End with a thank you.
Ending a conversation with a thank-you shows appreciation for the other person.

There are many ways to say thank you.

CHART

→ Thank you for sharing that with me.

→ Thank you for telling me.

→ Thank you for trusting me.

→ I appreciate it.

And there you have it -- the Communication C.L.U.E.

Choose positive words over negative ones.
Listen.
Use "I" instead of "you."
End with a thank you.

Communication Ninja was so happy to share the Communication C.L.U.E. with his friend.

He hoped it would help him communicate his feelings better.

Remembering the Communication C.L.U.E. could be your secret weapon against trouble with communication.

Choose.

Listen.

Use.

End.

Made in the USA
Las Vegas, NV
15 February 2021